OUTCASTS

For Sebastian David
Francesco Stone and
Evangeline Lilly Rose
Stone, my own little
heroes. This book is also
for Oliver and Daniela
Sereno-Spicer, whose
wedding inspired it.

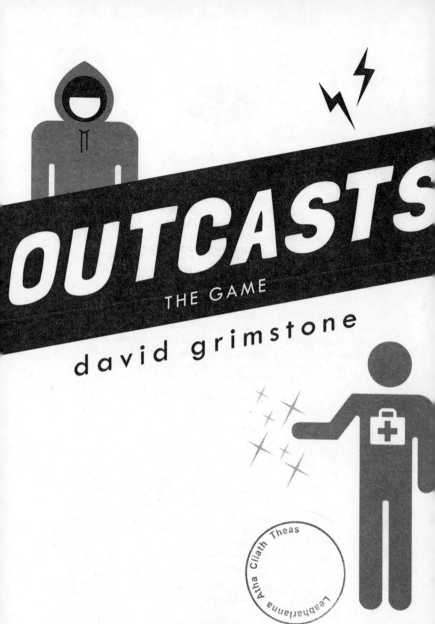

OUTCASTS

THE GAME

david grimstone

Hodder
Children's
Books

HODDER CHILDREN'S BOOKS

First published in Great Britain in 2016 by Hodder and Stoughton

Text copyright © David Grimstone, 2016
Inside illustrations © Shutterstock
Design by Lynne Manning
The moral rights of the author have been asserted.

A CIP catalogue record for this book
is available from the British Library.

ISBN 9781444925364

The paper and board used in this book
are made from wood from responsible sources.

Hodder Children's Books
An imprint of
Hachette Children's Group
Part of Hodder and Stoughton
Carmelite House
50 Victoria Embankment
London EC4Y 0DZ

An Hachette UK Company
www.hachette.co.uk

www.hachettechildrens.co.uk

CONTENTS

Pandora's Box is an artefact in Greek mythology, said to contain all the evils of the world. In modern usage, the phrase 'to open Pandora's Box' means to make a seemingly small mistake that causes chaos for everyone involved.

DO YOU LONG FOR A LIFE OF ADVENTURE?

ARE YOU TIRED OF SPENDING YOUR SUMMER HOLIDAYS JUST HANGING AROUND WITH NOTHING TO DO?

ARE YOU BRAVE OF HEART, STRONG OF PURPOSE AND NEVER AFRAID OF DANGER?

If the answer to all these questions is yes, then look no further – you have found your destiny.

Within this package lies the key to a world only YOU could imagine – the world of ...

 **DESTINY**

The **ULTIMATE FANTASY** role-playing game for ages 10-adult.

THE ONLY LIMIT ... IS THE POWER OF YOUR CREATIVITY!

1

The Outcasts

Looking back, Jake Cherish could never remember actually buying the box. He could only remember pointing at it and walking out of the shop with the thing wedged under his arm.

He'd been to Butter's Game Shop many times before and, like every teenager in Mendlesham, he knew the rule: you didn't talk to Stew about games – especially not on a Saturday morning.

Stew Butter was a nice enough

guy, but he absolutely *lived* for games: computer games, board games, card games, you name it he played it. His particular favourites were fantasy role-playing games, and you could make no greater mistake than raising your eyebrows and asking: 'Any good?'

Stew had played everything from *Dungeons and Dragons* to *Call of Cthulhu*, and could tell you stories that chewed up a Saturday morning and spat it out. Before you knew it, you'd no-showed for a kickabout in the park and had five missed calls from your mum because you were late for lunch. There were so many stories: the time he faced the seven-headed dragon of Armin-Wrath, the night he fought goblins off the bridge at Moon Valley and even that fateful day he'd thrown down his invisibility cloak to go head to head with the Harpies of Narrow Death Rise.

Jake had heard all these stories a thousand times, but it never stopped him going into the shop. Stew Butter's Game Shop was magic, pure magic, and on a Saturday morning in Mendlesham, there was no better place to be. Shelves piled high with boxes promising *hours of fun and mayhem* nestled between glass cabinets containing row upon row of brightly painted miniatures: ogres, trolls, vampires, werewolves and demons. Occasionally, there was even a dragon, though these were usually priced far beyond the reach of pocket money and never remained on display for very long.

Jake took another glance at the box as he walked home along the harbour. The accompanying leaflet announced: *Destiny – The Ultimate Role-playing Game*. It was certainly a catchy title, but the game itself looked a bit complicated – the rulebook was huge.

Jake liked reading, especially when there was a good story involving cool heroes and lots of action. He'd read something like three hundred books before his thirteenth birthday. On reflection, this was probably the reason he belonged to the Outcasts: reading might be tolerated at school, but if you got caught with a book in your spare time, you might as well go kiss the headmaster's shoes. It was different at his last school, but so were a lot of things. A patchy few years for his dad's business had forced the family to move from their old house in Meadowford.

Jake now went to St Mark's Secondary School, home to the Outcasts. There wasn't a leader of the group, exactly, but he was pretty sure Lemon had given them the name. Before that, they had just been a bunch of losers that hung around beside the mobile huts and tried hard not to be seen. There was Fatyak, Kellogg, Lemon and Jake. He'd joined the group last, but that never seemed to matter to anyone. The Outcasts didn't choose their own members. If you got beaten up by Todd Miller, or victimised by his evil witch of a girlfriend, you were in.

Todd Miller was the resident thug at St Mark's and he was far worse than anything you saw on TV. A head taller than any other kid in the year, he spent his time picking on everyone who didn't fit into his own idea of what a thug should look or act like. He also *named* people.

Fernando Reed had become Fatyak because he was overweight and, according to Todd Miller, smelled like an ox. Tom Frost was Kellogg because his mum had once packed him a fun-size box of Kellogg's Cornflakes every day for a week. In contrast, no one in the group had ever quite worked out why Lucy Anderson was Lemon.

Lucy was small, with short blonde hair and piercing blue eyes. She was a member of the Outcasts for two reasons: because Todd Miller's girlfriend didn't like her and because she always took a long time to answer people. Although this made her seem a bit slow, she was probably the smartest kid at St Mark's.

Jake's Miller-given name was Dealmo, because his dad owned a rundown garage called Deal Motors. The unfortunate thing was, Todd Miller's names stuck. Even the Outcasts called Jake 'Dealmo' and Lucy 'Lemon' for the simple reason that they had never known each other as anything else. Jake was in the group because he'd volunteered as Year Librarian two days after he joined St Mark's, a mistake that had drawn Todd Miller like a moth to a flame. A good thing, too. If Miller hadn't stolen his school bag and kicked him down the hill beside the H.E. Block, he might never have found the Outcasts ...

    ... or, rather, they might never have found him.

⚡

Jake cut through the alley by the shops and was surprised to see Fatyak dawdling towards him. Despite the fact that he'd known Fernando Reed for years, he always had to suppress a grin when he saw the boy move. It wasn't so much the speed, more the strange tendency of half-jogging, half-tripping; that and the look of determined effort on Fatyak's creased face.

    'Fatyak, my man,' Jake muttered,

walking past the breathless youth and spinning him around so that they were both moving in the same direction. He fished in his pocket and produced the leaflet from the game box. 'Take a look at this bad boy.'

'Destiny,' Fatyak read, his cheeks creasing up as he squinted at the scratchy writing. 'The Ultimate Fant— Oh, it's one of those. I can't believe you're trying to get us into this stuff again – the last time was a nightmare. You needed a maths degree to work out how to hit a goblin the size of a toadstool!'

'Yeah, I know … Just thought this sounded like fun. Would you help me talk the others into it? Lemon's always open to trying new stuff, but Kellogg might be a hard sell. Especially after last time.'

'Sure, whatever.'

'Good on you, Fatyak. How's it going, anyway? You chillin'?'

'Kinda.' Fatyak was never chilling; he was either watching TV or he was bored. Unfortunately for Fatyak, his parents were exactly the same. So the fact that he was out in the rain meant that they were inside, probably glued to some cooking show or soap opera.

'Where's the gang today?'

'Dunno,' said Fatyak. 'Let's go find out.'

The two friends emerged from the

alley and followed the new road until it bled into Shipley Park. There was no one in the play area, but they headed to the big sink tunnel half-buried beneath the slide.

Sure enough, Kellogg was huddled inside. He'd managed to find one tiny corner of the skeletal structure that still contained a fractured piece of roofing.

Kellogg always hung out in the park on Saturdays, because he had always played football with his dad on Saturdays. Kellogg's dad had died in a car accident nearly three years before, and was one of the nicest people Jake had ever met. Kellogg missed his dad terribly, and the Outcasts always got the feeling that whatever stuff they did together was only helping Kellogg to take his mind off things temporarily. Jake always felt guilty for being glad it wasn't *his* dad who'd died.

Kellogg was taller than Jake and ridiculously thin, as if he'd been stretched on a rack or some other torture device. His face was bony, and his hair always sopping with grease. Jake had wondered a few times if rainy days provided the only actual *wash* Kellogg's hair ever got. He was also bright, possibly even smarter than Lemon — and that took some doing.

Before they'd even ducked into the

pavilion, Kellogg had leapt to his feet.

'Dealmo, Fatyak – what's up?'

'Check this out!'

Jake gave a signal to Fatyak, who pressed the now damp leaflet into Kellogg's pale hands.

'Darkness and – oh, get out of here – another RPG? What is it with you and this stuff? It's *boring*.'

'Can't you just—'

'Rearrange these words into a well-known phrase: way no.'

'Stop being a twazzock.'

'I'm not being a twazzock. You two are being twazzockettes.'

'It does sound kinda cool,' Fatyak

added, glancing at Jake to see if this was enough in the way of support.

'Please, Kellogg,' said Jake. 'It will be something to do tomorrow night at Lemon's, rather than sitting in that stupid tree-house making up stories about Todd Miller and his dumb girlfriend.'

'You do this every time,' said Kellogg, resentfully. 'You go out and buy some stupid game thinking that we'll all have a laugh, but it's always me who has to read the rules and memorise everything. That last game was rubbish — I've never seen anything so complicated in my life. There were fourteen types of troll, all with different armour and weapons —

every fight took twenty minutes to get going.'

Jake shot Fatyak a look, but it seemed his friend was out of ammunition.

'Fine,' he snapped. 'I just wasted twenty quid on a game no one will play. It's not like I need the money or anything ...'

He reached out for the leaflet, but Kellogg quickly withdrew his hand.

'Alright! If you're gonna cry about it, I suppose we might as well break the thing open and lose another three hours of our lives in the mind of some warped game designer.'

Jake usually wanted to hit Kellogg three seconds after talking to him, but he was so happy to get the bony idiot on side that his face broke into a grin.

'Good on you, man,' said Fatyak, as Kellogg began to read the leaflet.

'Yeah,' Jake added. 'Lemon'll definitely want to play if we're all in – this should be a good laugh.'

Kellogg looked up, and rolled his eyes at them.

2

The Reach

In a candlelit room that ran off a sewage tunnel beneath the seaside town of Keyport, Colonel Bleach put down his pen and gave a small sigh.

Colonel Bleach had never been in the army, and his real surname wasn't remotely like Bleach. In fact, he had been given the identity for two simple reasons: he was a Colonel because it made people think he was part of a regulated service and he was Bleach because his main job was to clean up other people's mess. He was good at this.

Colonel Bleach belonged to an organisation called the Reach, an unregistered government splinter group retained to hunt down precious artefacts that many would consider the stuff of legend.

The sewer room was depressing — it was rat-infested and constantly dripping with things you had to try very hard not to look at. A shadow shifted in the corner of the room and Bleach immediately turned towards it.

You never heard Nathan Heed, and you certainly didn't see him — not until he wanted you to. By then, of course, it was probably too late to do anything other than scream.

Nathan Heed had joined the Reach when he was twelve years old and, although his upbringing was still something of a mystery, he had immediately been marked as special. His methods could be strange and he showed his enemies little or no mercy; he could be relied upon to find things other people couldn't.

Now, just three weeks away from his nineteenth birthday, he was the best agent working for the group.

'Good evening, Nathan.' Bleach smiled. 'Sorry to summon you at such a late hour. I trust I didn't interrupt anything important?'

Nathan Heed had a face like a child's drawing of a person; all the right bits were there but you couldn't look at it without asking who it was supposed to be. His eyes were pale and colourless, his lips thin and drawn. His hair, blond and needle straight, was so uneven that it appeared to have been cut with a beard-trimmer. He was short and slim, but by no means healthy-looking, and always gave the impression that he was about to nod off.

Heed blinked three times in quick succession; Bleach thought it might be the scariest thing he had ever seen. If it wasn't for the infinitely more terrifying employer they both reported to, Bleach would have been worried about keeping the younger man in line. A shudder ran through him as he remembered a promise he'd made to himself never to work with Nathan Heed after the last contract.

'I summoned you here for a very important mission,' he said, pouring himself some water from a small bottle on his desk. 'I need you to retrieve something.'

Heed said nothing, but his bony hands reached for the desk and rested there like two spiders ready to pounce.

He made no attempt to sit down.

'What is it, sir?'

'A box. A simple black box approximately the size and shape of a briefcase, though it may be disguised in some other way. It has recently found its way back into the public domain because a few of our former partners weren't quite as trustworthy as we thought.'

Colonel Bleach opened a brown, tea-stained folder.

'Nathan,' he began, talking very slowly and deliberately. 'This file contains the true story of Pandora's Box, and how it was handed down in secret through the generations, passing from country to country and, more recently, from order to order. We must get this artefact back, Nathan — our very survival as a group may depend upon it. They,' He glanced upwards, 'are depending on you.'

Heed nodded, and folded his arms.

'It will be back in your hands soon, Sir. You can be sure of that.

3

Destiny

Lemon's house was practically a mansion; her parents were both surgeons at some big London hospital, and it was obvious that the family was minted. Even the gnomes in the porch looked expensive. Still, Lemon's folks were nice enough, if a bit distant. They always spoke to you as if they'd just remembered something important that was happening a long way away. Kellogg called it 'Left the Gas on Syndrome'.

Jake hadn't been on the step for more than ten minutes when Fatyak's mum dropped him off in their battered estate car. She always looked angry whenever she had to give her son a lift, presumably because she was missing an episode of something and would have to go through the exhausting menu on catch-up TV. Jake looked away as Fatyak climbed out; he always laughed when the entire car sprang back up once relieved of Fatyak's weight, and he didn't want to risk his friend's wrath tonight. Fatyak pulled a sports bag after him, and dawdled up the front path while the estate roared away.

'Hey, Dealmo.'

'Hey yourself. Er ... your mum looked miffed ...'

'Yeah; she missed ten minutes of Eastenders, and we haven't got Sky TV yet. I think the bloke's coming to fit it on Friday.'

Jake laughed. There was *always* a bloke going to Fatyak's house on Friday. Sometimes he was fitting Sky TV, sometimes he was bringing Playstation or Xbox consoles and occasionally he was even delivering a new car. Jake didn't know why Fatyak couldn't just admit his family were poor; it wasn't as if he and Kellogg were loaded.

'Guys!'

Jake and Fatyak both saluted as Kellogg's bike hopped the drive hump and skidded to a halt on the gravel. Dismounting, Kellogg unhooked a carrier bag from the handlebars and walked the bike over to the front wall, where he chained it up.

'I read the rules to Destiny last night. You're right, Dealmo, it does sound better than the usual tripe. You can be a sorcerer, a master thief, a warrior or a holy acolyte, which is kind of like a magical priest. The sorcerer has this magical staff and a spell-book, the warrior has super strength, the thief can climb walls and steal practically anything from anyone, and the acolyte can call upon his gods for divine favour!'

'Bet Lemon likes it,' said Fatyak, as the Andersons' BMW rolled into the drive.

Mrs Anderson got out first, which invariably cracked the Outcasts up because her feet always hit the ground before the car had stopped moving. This provoked a glare from Mr Anderson that made the whole scene fifty times funnier.

Lemon was the last to emerge from the car, a dreamy look in her eyes which expired when they came to focus on the rest of the Outcasts.

'Oh – hello,' she said, pausing to take her customary breath between sentences. 'You guys are really early.'

'Sorry,' Jake muttered. 'We're all pretty eager to get going on this new game I bought.'

'No way.'

'Come on!'

'The last one was awful—'

'Come onnnnnnnnn!'

'No!'

Fatyak stepped between them. 'We've got Fizzback Exploders?' he said, pulling the sweets from his pocket.

Lemon looked down, and grinned.

'M'kay,' she said. 'I'm in.'

Lemon's parents had built her a tree-house for her eleventh birthday. At least, that's what they said. In fact, they had gone on a business trip to New York on Lemon's eleventh birthday, and had paid for some workmen to build a tree-house while her uncle and aunt stayed with her. Mr and Mrs Anderson seemed to do that sort of thing a lot: buy stuff to make up for not actually being there. Jake envied Lemon the expensive gifts, but thought he'd probably feel differently if he were in her shoes.

Kellogg snatched Jake's backpack and raced ahead of the group, waving his arms and screaming a strangled war-cry. By the time Jake, Lemon and (eventually) Fatyak heaved themselves through the trapdoor and into the tree-house, Kellogg was already unpacking the game.

'Did you buy this new or second-hand?' he asked, staring down at the open box with a puzzled expression on his face.

'New! I got it from Butter's. What's wrong with it?'

Kellogg frowned again. 'There's supposed to be three six-sided dice with it. Instead, there's only one taped to the main rulebook ... and it's only got four sides. The rulebook looks totally different to the box, and there's a load of maps and floor-plans missing, too.'

'Seriously?' Jake scowled. Lemon wordlessly went to the house and raided her dad's Monopoly box. When she returned, Jake was looking at one of the small triangular dice Fatyak was holding between his chubby fingers. 'If we can't play it, I'll complain,' Jake said. 'I have his mobile number.'

Kellogg shrugged. 'We can play it, but — I dunno. The box is wooden: that's odd for an RPG. Also, the insides are, like, carved out. It's all a bit ... plain. If you remember Dungeons of—'

'Can we just play?' Fatyak cut in.

'I want to see who gets who.'

'OK,' Kellogg conceded. 'We're supposed to roll in order of age, so Dealmo goes first, followed by Lemon and then Fatyak. I'll take whichever character is left. Dealmo, roll the dice inside the box!'

Jake made a face, picked up two of the six-sided dice Lemon had retrieved from the house and threw them into the wooden container.

'I got a ten. What does that mean?'

Kellogg turned a page and ran his finger down a graph of some kind.

'Depends. What star sign are you?'

'What, in real life?'

'Yeah.'

Jake's brow creased into a frown. 'I'm Scorpio.'

'Right ...' Kellogg cross-referenced the star sign with the previous result, and smiled broadly. 'You're the sorcerer,' he said.

'What?' Jake rolled his eyes and slumped back against the wall of the tree-house. 'I hate wizards — I wanted to be a fighter! Now I'm going to have the strength of a gnat and I bet I have to learn a bunch of stupid spells off by heart.'

'I'm Scorpio, too.'

'Eh?' Kellogg looked at Fatyak

with one eyebrow raised.

'I said I'm Scorpio, too. So if I roll a ten, surely I'm going to be another sorcerer?'

Kellogg turned a new page in the rulebook and shook his head. 'If the wizard is taken, we move onto a new chart.'

Five minutes later, everyone in the tree-house was disappointed.

Lemon had fared no better than Jake. She'd set her sights on the holy acolyte, mainly because that way she got to heal people who were hurt and create things like circles of light and protection. She'd ended up with a super-strong warrior princess who could lift drawbridges with her bare hands, pull broadswords from magical rocks and wrestle sabre-toothed tigers to the ground.

The others laughed at this idea, as they were always talking about Lemon's temper and the fact that, one day, she'd finally lose it with Todd Miller's catty girlfriend and rugby-tackle her on the school playing-field.

Fatyak was probably more miserable than anyone else. He'd drawn the thief, a nimble-footed lord of shadows who was never seen and seldom heard — unlike Fatyak himself, who you probably wouldn't miss if he was three streets away.

Kellogg had been saddled with the holy acolyte, a character he didn't want partly because he didn't like priests, but mostly because he had been a holy acolyte in every RPG the Outcasts had ever played.

'OK,' Kellogg said, turning yet another page in the rulebook and clearing his throat. 'Before you actually get to play your character, it says that we need to make The Sacred Oath.'

'Terrific,' said Jake, his voice lacking any of the enthusiasm he had previously felt. 'How do we do that?

'I'm guessing you put your hand in here, right?' Lemon held up the wooden box; inside the lid was an imprint of a hand. 'I found a clasp underneath the lid,' Lemon explained. 'When you push it, the top layer folds back and there's this handprint inside.'

'Wow,' muttered Fatyak. 'That's pretty cool.'

Jake nodded in agreement. 'Yeah; neat idea. Haven't seen anything like that in an RPG before.'

When silence settled again, everyone looked at Kellogg, who had returned his attention to the rulebook and was scanning each page with a puzzled look on his face.

'It doesn't say anything about a handprint,' he said. 'It just says the words you need to say to make each character's oath. I guess the handprint makes it all more authentic.'

Kellogg gave the book to Jake, and everyone waited a few seconds for Jake to place his hand in the handprint and read through the lines.

'Right, er ... I am the sorcerer, a powerful conjurer of magical objects and mystical energies. With this hand, I make the pledge and ask the gods to give me wisdom.'

Everyone laughed as Jake made

an expression that he felt resembled the face of a man given wisdom by the gods.

'OK,' said Lemon, taking the rulebook and placing her own hand inside the handprint. 'I am the warrior, a mighty mercenary skilled in the art of combat. With this hand, I make the pledge and ask the gods to give me might.'

'I am the master thief,' said Fatyak, in his turn. 'A wily cutpurse of devastating skill and extraordinary talent. With this hand, I make the pledge and ask the gods to give me stealth.'

'And last but not least,' said Kellogg, placing his hand inside the box and half closing his eyes. 'I am the holy acolyte, a servant of the divine and a healer of ills. With this hand, I make the pledge and ask the gods to give me favour.'

Kellogg grinned, snatched up the rulebook and opened it at a new section. 'Right,' he said. 'Let's play. You three are all on the outskirts of the city of, er, whatever, and because of the evil Baron's permanent lockdown system, the only way you can actually get in is via the sewers. Everybody clear on that?'

There was a series of nods and positive murmurs, so Kellogg continued: 'The sewers are a maze of stinking tunnels crawling with all manner of evil creatures and some pretty unfriendly magic. You are currently looking for the sewer guardian, a powerful gnome-wraith. He hangs around in some of the darker tunnels, tormenting travellers and – just occasionally – leading a lucky few into the city.'

Fatyak yawned. 'Why does he lead travellers into the city? Doesn't he have anything better to do with his time? I mean, if he's got magical powers and stuff, why does he hang around a sewer?'

Jake and Lemon shared a glance, but it seemed that Fatyak was far from satisfied.

'Can we find a way into the city without this idiot?' he continued.

'My thief is searching the tunnels for a secret door, and I mean every brick in every wall.'

Kellogg looked up from the rulebook. 'That's ridiculous, you can't check every brick — you'd be down there for the rest of your life! You can do a basic search. But when you step forward to try there is a flash of light and a small gnome appears before you. He introduces himself as Erol Winesock, and tells you that you will most likely be trapped or killed in the sewer.'

'Can he help us?' Lemon asked. 'Offer him gold or something. Do we have money?'

'He says he isn't interested in gold,' Kellogg advised them. 'Instead, he asks you to prove your worth to him by demonstrating your heroic abilities. If he considers you an asset to the city, he will lead you to the secret entrance.'

Jake rolled his eyes. 'Right, I'm going to hold out my hand and try to conjure something out of thin air: that should impress him, shouldn't it?'

'Sure,' said Kellogg. 'What exactly are you hoping for? If it's something small, you only need to roll a three. But if it's something bigger ...'

'Yeah, I know.' Jake frowned. 'I'm going to conjure a frog – no, a toad!

That's it! I'm going to conjure one of those mega toads!'

Jake held out his right hand and began to mutter a fake incantation, full of words like mojo, hoodoo and abracadabra. Then he closed his eyes and rolled the dice.

It rattled to a halt, and a grim silence invaded the tree-house.

Nobody moved.

'I'm not even going to look,' Jake said, one hand closed over his eyes. 'What did I get? It's a one isn't it?'

When no one answered, Jake opened his eyes. Fatyak, Lemon and Kellogg were all staring at him, open-mouthed. Fatyak had dropped his packet of onion rings onto the floor, Kellogg had let go of the rulebook and Lemon was simply aghast.

Jake followed their combined gaze and looked down at his hand. Hovering over his palm was a fat, warty toad. A real one. It floated down onto his skin.

'Ribbit,' it croaked.

Lemon screamed. Fatyak gawped. Kellogg opened and shut his mouth without speaking.

Jake gave a little yelp of surprise, dropping the toad as if it was charged with electric. The warty visitor tried to leap past Lemon, but she instinctively shot out a hand and snatched it up.

'W-which one of you did this?'

'No one,' said Lemon, raising her hands to show everybody the toad that was resting quite comfortably while looking ever so slightly put out. 'We saw it, Dealmo. It just appeared.'

'She's right,' Fatyak added. 'One second you were holding out your hand and the next there was a toad in it! There wasn't a puff of smoke or a bolt of energy or anything.'

'B-b-but that's totally impossible!'

'Hmm …' Kellogg nodded. 'It is. Unless you really are a sorcerer.'

Lemon and Fatyak looked at Jake

with sudden awe, but if anything this shook him from his reverie and finally made him laugh.

'Oh, don't be ridiculous!' he said. 'I wasn't a sorcerer yesterday when Mum asked me to tidy my room. I wasn't a sorcerer on Wednesday morning when Todd Miller nicked my school-bag after Gym and belted me over the head with it. How come I'm suddenly a wiz—'

'Sorry to interrupt,' said Lemon. The boys all turned to look at her. There were few things in life you could rely on, but Lemon's brain was one of them. When she said things like 'sorry to interrupt,' the chances were she had thought of something very important to say. 'I don't mean to put a downer on the amazing event that just happened, but role-playing games are for the imagination only — they don't actually turn people into the characters they play. Besides, the publishers produce hundreds each year. If a bunch of smart designers had created a fantasy game that actually gave people magical powers, I think there'd be something about it on the news. You know, like people creating toads, turning invisible or whirling up thunderstorms?'

Jake and Fatyak nodded in agreement, but Kellogg was visibly annoyed.

'Alright, then,' he said. 'But if it's not the game, what is it? Toads don't just *appear!*'

Lemon reached up and deposited the toad on a branch next to the window.

'I think,' she said, crawling over to where Kellogg was sitting and grabbing the box. 'That this is responsible. Not the game – *the box.*'

'The box isn't part of the game,' Jake said, suddenly meeting Lemon's gaze. 'The dice weren't in the box, and all the maps and floor-plans were missing.'

Kellogg slowly nodded. 'Everything was taped to the rulebook,' he said. 'Lemon's right – the box and the game don't go together. It's almost as if someone wrapped a shiny cover over this thing by mistake.'

Jake took the box from Lemon and turned it over in his hands. It did seem odd, he had to admit. Then again, most of the things in Stew Butter's game shop were a bit strange.

'It does look like it's about five million years old,' he hazarded.

'There's also the handprint,' Kellogg chimed in. 'What if the box is some kind of ancient wizard's chest that grants wishes—'

'What wishes?' said Jake, looking down at his hands. 'I didn't even make a wish!'

'Yes you did,' Lemon corrected him. 'You made an oath and in that oath you asked the gods to turn you into a sorcerer.'

'But that was just game talk!'

'Maybe the box doesn't know that,' said Kellogg. He gulped, and a sudden mixture of fear and excitement filled the room. 'Maybe you *did* make a wish and maybe that wish was granted. What if you really are a sorcerer now? Try something else!'

'Like what?'

Kellogg shrugged. 'I don't know … an energy bolt or something?'

'That's a bit drastic,' said Lemon. 'I think he should go for an apple. That way, we can taste it and see if it's normal.'

'There was nothing normal about that toad.'

'No,' said Lemon, carefully, 'but it was a giant toad and that was exactly what he asked for.'

'Go ahead, Dealmo,' Kellogg muttered.

Jake closed his eyes and began to focus his mind. This time, however, he felt the weight of the apple as it appeared in his hand. He also heard the combined gasps of the Outcasts as he opened his eyes to another miracle.

'Wow!'

'Amazing!'

'That's epic!'

Jake grinned, and took a bite from the apple. 'It's really good,' he said, swallowing the mouthful and throwing the rest aside. 'Now I'll go for an orange. Drum roll, please!'

Jake closed his eyes again. Unfortunately, before he could conjure anything, Kellogg swore rather loudly and broke his concentration.

Kellogg was staring up at the ceiling, open-mouthed. Jake followed his gaze. At first, he thought Fatyak was flying. Then he looked down, and saw that the heaviest member of the Outcasts was being supported on the tip of Lemon's index finger.

4

Reflections

The stockroom was full of cracked and broken mirrors. Next door, on the other side of a plush red curtain, was Pip Duncan's magnificent show hall, where a selection of the most beautiful mirrors in Shipley hung on display.

Twenty minutes before, the stockroom had been full of mirrors, but none were cracked and very few were broken. *Nineteen* minutes before, the shop had been entered by two men who had proceeded to lock the front door, drag the owner behind the plush curtain and push him into every mirror in the room.

The taller of the two, who had slick blond hair and was shaped like a mountain gorilla, fished in his pocket and produced a roll of tape. He tore into it with his teeth and wrapped a strip around the lower half of his victim's pale face.

His partner, a good head shorter with greying hair and a patchwork of scars on his face, took a file from his pocket and used it to scrape his fingernails.

'Which one they sending, Clax?'

'The worst one, Sluddy. The worst

one.' The older man ran a hand through his thinning hair and moved over to unlatch the back door. Peering out, he could see no sign of movement but that didn't mean anything. He went back inside, ignoring the frown that was threatening to consume his partner's forehead.

'Afternoon, people,' said Nathan Heed, stepping from the shadows and crunching across the glass as if he'd been present through the entire operation. He was wearing silver shades, a bright white shirt and a pair of ripped denim jeans. Crouching beside the prone figure, he slapped the man in order to wake him up.

'A Fairy Tale,' Heed said, grabbing Pip by the throat and ripping the tape from his mouth. 'Once upon a time, in a land not too far away, there lived a man who made a bad decision. His name was Ingold, and he stole a special piece of treasure from some extremely ruthless people. He's gone now, but before he left he muttered one name, loudly and very clearly. PIP DUNCAN.'

'P-p-please!' cried the man, trying to wriggle free of the iron hand that was clamped around his wrinkled neck. 'D-don't kill me! I didn't know how important it was!' Duncan coughed as Heed released his grip. 'I swear on my—'

'WHERE is it?'

Duncan stared at Nathan Heed, but said nothing. It was as if he couldn't bring himself to believe that things could get any worse. He was wrong.

'Did you ever watch *Blockbusters*, Mr Duncan?' Reach's best agent continued, cracking his knuckles. 'It has questions like this: what B, who is your oldest friend, has – I'm guessing – recently received a very special present from his bezzie mate, Pip Duncan?'

Duncan lowered his head and began to sob: deep, booming wails that made even Claxon look down at his shoes.

'You don't know the answer?' Heed produced a small case, unclasped the lid and removed a small glass container. Inside, a tiny green snake wriggled back and forth. It immediately drew Pip Duncan's undivided attention.

'This little specimen is an Inland Taipan,' Heed started, turning the container slightly so that the snake had to wriggle in order to stop itself slipping. 'It's one of the most deadly snakes known to mankind; a single bite from an adult Taipan contains enough venom to kill a quarter of a million mice ... or approximately one hundred humans. Now, this one here is only a *baby* but I'd be amazed if it didn't have enough juice to put down one ageing shopkeeper.' Heed smiled and put the small container on the floor beside him, uncorking the stopper and stowing it inside his pocket. 'I'll ask again: what B is the name of a friend who is actually worth dying for?'

'Butter!' the man spat, so loudly that Claxon and Slud started. 'Stew Butter!'

'What a lovely name,' Heed repeated, licking his lips. 'It may surprise you to know that I am acquainted with Mr Butter, as he was once a member of our *select* organisation. Sadly, we've lost touch. So, I have to ask, where exactly has Mr Butter got to with our very special property? We know he's not at his pathetic game shop, because we've already been there. Now, do talk quickly, Pip, before one of us dies.'

'R-Rochester! He's in a flat beside the cathedral, over the top of a bakery! He's got a gang of roughs protecting him!'

Nathan Heed smiled again. 'Has he indeed?'

5

Keeping Secrets

It was fast approaching midnight, but the sleeping bags Lemon's parents had left for the Outcasts still lay rolled up at the foot of the giant oak tree that supported the tree-house.

'Let's get this straight,' Jake was saying, trying to keep the increasing excitement out of his voice. 'Lemon has the strength of twenty men, Fatyak can blend in with walls and climb trees like a spider, *you* can heal wounds like the one we just carved in my arm ...'

'... and you can conjure pretty much anything out of thin air,' Kellogg finished. 'Cool – now we've got all that sorted out, who's up for a visit to Todd Miller's house?'

There was a small eruption of awkward laughter, but in truth everyone apart from Kellogg was too nervous to joke.

'I don't believe this,' said Jake, rubbing his unblemished arm that had been pouring with blood mere seconds before. 'I know I keep saying it over and over again, but I really do not believe this. I mean – what on earth are we going to do?'

'The responsible thing,' said Lemon, putting on her most concerned frown when the boys all looked at her as if she'd gone insane. 'Whenever you watch a film where kids get special powers, they always make the same mistake. They go mental. We should do the opposite.'

'I can hide in plain sight,' Fatyak said, dreamily. 'I could sneak round to Emily Jacob's house and hide in her bathroom ...'

'That's sick,' Lemon snapped. 'Besides, you're stealthy – not invisible.'

'Do you think I can heal sick people?' said Kellogg, trying not to think of his dad lying in the hospital bed after the accident. 'I mean, people with terminal diseases and stuff?'

Jake nodded. 'You might be able to. You asked the gods for favour. That might mean you can pretty much save anybody from anything ...'

'That's a much more useful gift than mine,' Lemon reflected. 'I'm like Superman, but without the eye-lasers or the ability to fly. I suppose I'd come in handy if someone was jammed under a bus or if a group of businessmen got stuck in a lift, but apart from that I really don't see how—'

'Bet you're amazing with a sword,'

Jake hazarded, trying to cheer her up. 'I bet you can even do that Web of Death move Arnie does in the Conan films.'

Lemon flushed at the compliment, quickly changing the subject to Jake's own abilities.

'You're the one who really lucked in,' she said. 'You can probably conjure anything.'

Jake tried to shrug the statement off. 'That still doesn't answer the most important question about all this. If we're not going to end up like every kid in the movies with magic powers, what are we actually going to do?'

'Nothing,' said Kellogg, decisively.

Everyone looked at him.

'Er ... nothing?' said Fatyak. 'How do you mean, exactly?'

'Yeah,' Jake added. 'What's the point of having special powers if you don't use them? Isn't that like owning a really fast car and walking everywhere?'

Kellogg jumped to his feet and began to pace back and forth. 'You see, this is it!' he yelled. 'The same conversation that always leads to disaster in the films.' He pursed his lips and put on a squeaky voice: '*What's the point of having special powers if you're not going to use them?* The next minute, everyone except the main kid is dead, and *he's* in a lunatic asylum.'

'So what?' Jake snapped back. 'Lemon goes to school every day and just ignores the fact that she can punch a hole in the side of the science labs if she wanted to? I listen to my parents screaming at each other downstairs when I know I could probably click my fingers for a pair of really enormous earmuffs?'

'Shut up, Dealmo,' Kellogg warned, but his tone irritated Jake and he ploughed on.

'I'm serious, man. What happens in gym class when Fatyak suddenly shins up the ropes like a spider monkey? We all laugh it off and say he's been on a really weird diet that doesn't actually affect your weight?'

Only Fatyak seemed to see the funny side of this; Lemon and Kellogg were both getting angry.

'You're *always* like this, Dealmo,' Kellogg muttered. 'You can never see the positive side of anything. You just have to dwell on the bad stuff ...'

'Yeah?' Jake got to his feet and strode up to Kellogg, until the two friends' faces were inches apart. 'How exactly are *you* being positive? You were just saying how we're all going to end up dead or in a lunatic asylum!'

'Oi!' Fatyak shouted. 'What's

wrong with you, Dealmo?'

Jake didn't even pause. He snatched up the heavy sports bag Fatyak had brought along and hurled it across the tree-house with all his might.

Fatyak leapt aside, somersaulting twice before he hit the wall and rebounded into a crouching position. Jake immediately turned his attention to Lemon, and aimed a punch straight at her face. She blocked the strike and closed her fist around his hand like a vice, but he twisted away, catching Kellogg in the face with the back of his other hand.

The boy's head snapped back and he staggered slightly, a look of sudden astonishment on his face. Then he rounded on his friend like an angry lion.

'What in seven hells is up with you, Dealmo?' he managed. A stream of blood ran from his nose, but thinned quickly before stopping. 'Have you gone completely crazy?'

It was Lemon who answered.

'No,' she said. 'He's not gone crazy at all. Dealmo is proving that we *will* use these powers, when we're forced to. It's like a natural defence.'

'Exactly,' said Jake, straightening himself up. 'You protect yourself like you always do in a bad situation, only now you can do it a whole lot better with very little effort.' He dawdled back to Kellogg and threw an apologetic hug around his friend's shoulder. 'I'm just trying to prove that if we want to keep this stuff quiet, we're going to have to work at it.'

'So, just to be sure,' Lemon said. 'Nobody thinks we should try to give this back?' She looked around at a sea of doubtful and confused expressions. 'You know, the box, the powers ... everything.'

Kellogg shook his head. 'What if we can't put them back? We might end up behind bars, or as experiments in some freaky science lab?'

'We keep the powers,' Jake muttered. 'At least we're all decent people. Can you imagine what would happen if someone like Todd Miller was in our place?'

🗲

In the days that had passed since the Outcasts discovered their strange new powers, a contented calm had settled over the group.

Fatyak had been particularly attentive to Lemon's advice about using their powers unnecessarily and, if anything, was putting on a display of being even worse at PE than normal. Kellogg hadn't found his own gift all that difficult to hide, and managed to restrain himself when a girl he really fancied cut her leg quite badly in one of the science labs. As usual, Lemon was the most measured of the group, not even rising to the bait when Todd Miller's evil girlfriend tripped her up at lunch and cackled as Lemon went face-first into a table of fourth-years.

Jake, on the other hand, was finding their new secret increasingly difficult to hide as he developed an understanding of his powers. At home, he regularly conjured food when the cupboards were empty, at school he would summon up the occasional rat in the Home Economics block, which invariably resulted in a free period just after lunch. Suffice to say, the other members of the Outcasts were not impressed.

Lemon's tree-house had become an even more appealing hide-out for the group than usual. They met there every day at six o'clock, and would generally idle away an hour or two showing off some new skill they had, then argue about who should keep hold of the box. This was becoming a feature of almost every meeting.

The box, it was decided, was dangerous. It was also precious, and on no account to be toyed with unless everyone was present. Kellogg had successfully argued that the box should be buried until they knew more about it, and he and Fatyak had put forward the idea of digging a hole somewhere in Lemon's garden near the tree-house. This had been agreed by the other Outcasts, and the box had been buried beneath a rose bush mere feet from the base of the tree. Nevertheless, their worries about its power continued to intensify, and an unexpected confrontation was about to make everything much more difficult to hide.

6
The Storm

It happened when Kellogg and Lemon were walking home from school. They walked home together most nights, as they only lived two streets apart. As usual, they'd taken a detour through the parade to grab a couple of ice creams at Chaser's kiosk. Unfortunately, two very familiar voices rang out a few metres away from their destination.

'It's the Kellogg's Cornflake!' shouted Todd Miller, striding over towards the pair and motioning for the rest of his rag-tag mob to dawdle in the same direction. 'And what's this? His oh-so-tasty girlfriend, Lemsip.'

'Ignore him,' Lemon advised, stepping around Kellogg in order to join the kiosk queue. 'He'll get bored and bother someone else.'

'Yeah, *just ignore me*,' Miller imitated. He brought his head forward until it was mere inches from Kellogg's. 'If you can, Cornflake.'

Lemon glanced around to see if any of the adults in the kiosk queue would try to help, but it was immediately obvious that they didn't want to get involved.

'You ignoring me OK, Cornflake?' Miller persisted, getting right in Kellogg's face as three of his mates mooched over to join them. 'Hey guys, I'm just helping Kellogg here to ignore me so I'll go away … isn't that right, Cornflake?'

Lemon stepped out of the queue and moved to stand between the boys, forcing Todd Miller to take a step back.

'Whoah! Looky here – Lemsip's protecting her wimpy boyfriend from the evil forces of—'

'Shut your mouth.'

The statement was snapped off so quickly that Miller's cronies looked momentarily doubtful that it had actually come from the girl.

Todd Miller's expression changed slightly, and he shoved Lemon aside.

'I asked you a question, Cornflake. Have you gone deaf or something?'

It happened so fast that not even Kellogg, who was standing right in the middle of the group, could describe the strike.

One of Todd's cronies, a tall kid with wavy blond hair and a huge nose, went flying backwards as if he'd been caught on a phantom wind. He hurtled into one of the larger tables that surrounded the kiosk, rolled over the surface and landed with a comical thud on the grass verge behind. He quickly jumped to his feet, staggered sideways and collapsed, a dazed expression on his face.

'What the hell?' Todd Miller looked over at his friend, flashing a smirk that quickly vanished when his eyes met Lemon's. 'Don't even think about pretending that was you,' he said.

'I don't need to think about it,' said Lemon, as Todd's remaining cronies began to shrink away. 'I can just demonstrate again by throwing you through a brick wall.'

Kellogg almost couldn't believe his eyes when Miller actually took a swing at Lemon.

Lemon snapped her hand around Todd Miller's fist as if she was catching a tennis ball and squeezed so hard that his entire arm turned white. She used the pressure to bear down on him, forcing the boy to his knees.

'I don't want to see you any more, Todd Miller,' she said, gritting her teeth and spitting the words at him. 'None of us do; not Dealmo, not Fatyak, not Kellogg and not me. Right now your so-called friends—' she indicated the fast receding shapes of Miller's crew '—are running off in all directions to tell everyone that their mighty leader just took a beating from a *girl*. That's cool, though, because at least you'll have learned your lesson and I might not have to do this in front of the entire school.'

Miller yelped as Lemon finally let go of him. He cradled his throbbing hand, trying frantically to massage some life back into his purple fingers.

'One warning, Miller,' said Lemon, as she rejoined the startled adults in the kiosk queue. 'And you better have listened, because one warning is all you'll ever get.'

'You tell him, dear,' said the old woman who'd been serving ice cream at the kiosk window. 'He smashed up one of my tables last weekend, that one, little hooligan. It's nice to see a young girl standing up for herself.'

Lemon nodded, ignoring her companion's startled expression. 'Thank you very much,' she said. 'Hmm … can I have two flake ice creams and a lemon doughnut, please?'

Kellogg had watched the entire scene unfold as if he was in the front row at the local cinema. It wasn't until he came to recount the day's events to Dealmo and Fatyak that he began to believe the incredible thing he'd witnessed.

Interestingly enough, when they met up at the tree-house that night, Dealmo and Fatyak had an incredible story of their own.

A storm was brewing ...

'You did *what*?' Lemon leapt up from the tree-house floor, glaring at Jake as if he'd just insulted her. 'Dealmo — you're the absolute height of immaturity, do you know that? It's like dealing with a little kid sometimes!'

'It was just a storm,' said Jake, defensively. 'Fatyak asked me if I could do them.'

'Oh great, blame *me*.'

'And I just thought I'd see if I could actually *control* the lightning. It didn't do any harm, Lemon. Plus, the whole storm only lasted about fifteen minutes from beginning to end.'

Kellogg rolled his eyes. 'We know *that*, Jake; we got caught in the thing. The rain was practically torrential.'

'How do you *know* it didn't do any damage?' Lemon persisted.

'Eh?' said Jake, frowning. 'What do you mean by that?'

'Well, the storm was over the entire town and you two were only in the park. So how do you actually *know* it didn't do any damage? Like striking down an old lady or a toddler playing football or something? Maybe it hit an aerial and fried somebody's TV set? Did you think of all that stuff? Of course you didn't — you just wanted to test your *amazing powers* ...'

'And you didn't?' Jake snapped back. 'Throwing Todd Miller's mates all over the kiosk tables and then crushing his jaw in front of a queue of adults? Real smart, Lemon — I can see why you're the club's major thinker.'

Lemon stormed towards Jake, causing the boy to take several steps back. His shoulders bumped the treehouse wall.

'Don't start with me, Dealmo,' she threatened, her eyes darkening, her hands clenching into fists.

'Or what?' Jake asked. 'You'll break *my* jaw and throw me out of your tree?'

Fatyak and Kellogg leapt to their feet, trying to force themselves between their friends before the situation got any worse.

'C'mon, Lemon,' Jake continued. 'I'm just saying that it's a bit rich having a go at me for the *possibility* of hurting people when you *actually* did hurt people.'

'It was *Todd Miller* and his cronies,' Lemon snapped. 'They beat us up a lot, remember? You, especially. I seem to remember they almost put you in hospital once when Miller loosened all the nuts on your bike. Then there was the time he sprayed that fake mist in Fatyak's eyes and we had to spend an entire *morning* washing them out with Opticon. You must have a really short memory, Dealmo.'

'Yeah, well,' Jake visibly deflated, withered under his friend's determined stare. 'What about keeping our gifts a secret, eh? How many people at that kiosk will go home and tell their families about the incredible girl with the *grip of steel* ...'

Lemon's expression remained dark, but her lips twitched slightly and, for the briefest of seconds, Kellogg and Fatyak thought she might burst out laughing.

'Alright,' she said eventually, 'we *both* did wrong. From now on, we need to agree *not* to rise to the temptation of using our powers for things that aren't emergencies. If I used my strength every time I was upset, the house would be a big pile of rubble today.'

'Why? What's up?'

'My parents are going to New York for Christmas,' Lemon said, 'and they're leaving me behind. I sometimes think they never even wanted me. They just do whatever they like and I'm left with some amazingly expensive present that,' she raised her voice and imitated her mother's weird accent, '*any other girl would be grateful for.'*

Jake opened and shut his mouth a few times, as if he was suddenly unsure of what he wanted to say.

'My sister is coming down from Scotland to stay in the house, but she only ever wants to see her old friends when she gets back; I bet she ends up going to parties every night. I-I just don't want to be on my own at Christmas.'

'You won't be,' said Kellogg, determinedly. 'We'll be right here.'

Jake nodded. 'We'll hang out on Christmas Eve *and* Christmas Day. I could probably manage Boxing Day, too.'

'Yeah,' added Fatyak. 'Count me

in; my mum and dad pretty much slob out after I open my presents on Christmas morning. We sometimes have a meal on Boxing Day, but they're going to some do at the Working Men's Club this year. I don't think they'd care if I didn't go with them.'

'Thanks, guys.' Lemon beamed at them, her eyes welling up with tears. 'You're the best friends a girl could have.'

7

Melting Butter

Don't answer the door.

It was a simple instruction, and one — Butter felt — even stupid people could follow.

No matter how many times the bell rings, do not under any circumstances open that door.

The problem was that seventy-five pounds a day didn't buy you clever men — it bought you thugs.

Butter practically swallowed his

tongue when the first crash erupted through the flat, but being an incredibly quick thinker, he was on his feet before the sounds of fighting broke out from below.

Sending the raft of text messages he'd been writing on his mobile, Butter leapt up from the sofa, crossed the room in two giant strides and half-crashed, half-fell into the small kitchen at the back of the flat. Getting to his feet, he snatched up a chair, whirled around and smashed the kitchen window, sending a shower of glass onto the roof of a bathroom that belonged to the flat below. Two seconds later, he was out of the room and sliding down the drainpipe at the back of the building, as the cacophonous noise of the smashed window brought several locals to their bedroom windows.

In the looming shadow cast by the cathedral, Butter crossed the rear courtyard in a pool of moonlight. He'd purposely left the back door unlatched for such an occasion and, as he dashed along the rubbish-strewn alley, he'd never been more grateful for his magnificent attention to detail.

As he emerged beneath a dim streetlight, a vehicle skidded to a halt beside the mouth of the alley, expelling a man the size of a polar bear who began to walk towards him as if taking a stroll in the park.

Butter doubled back, tripping as he went. He kicked a cat that got under his feet but managed not to collide with two dustbins as he desperately attempted to escape the giant that stalked him.

Butter was a slight and very fit man, and he ran with every ounce of energy that was available to him. Scooting out from the opposite end of the alley, he quickly dashed in a zigzag across the new street, taking a left turn at the first junction before darting through a second alleyway and arriving, nearly breathless, at the door of his car.

Still peering over his shoulder at two-second intervals, Butter snaked a hand under the front wheel-arch and grabbed the spare set of keys he always kept there. He pressed the remote, failing to notice that the car was already unlocked, and climbed inside ...

... where his heart nearly stopped.

A pale figure was sitting in the passenger seat beside him.

'If it isn't my old friend Butter,' said Nathan Heed, turning his head very slowly as if it was fixed on a pole. 'Nice of you to drop in.'

Heed flung out his arm in a blur. Butter felt his body shutting down.

His arms dropped to his sides and his legs splayed out as if he'd been given a paralysing drug.

'I need to talk to you, Mr Butter,' said Heed, an amused expression on his face. 'And since I can't have you running away, I thought a small sensory shock might cure you of any stupid ideas.'

Heed fished in his case and produced an antique but functional looking syringe. It was filled with a luminous green liquid.

'Ah yes, here we are. Now ... unless you tell me what I want to know I'm going to stick this needle into your neck, and, to make life interesting, I'm not even going to tell you what's in it ...'

'W-w-wait,' said Butter, trying and failing to lift his arms. He knew from experience that it was futile to withhold information from Heed. 'I'll t-t-tell you what I—'

'No.' Heed shook his head. 'Wait a few moments until you can move *and* speak properly again. I have paralysed you, rather than cause you pain. If you move *anything* apart from your mouth, I will make every tiny part of you explode in agony.'

Heed straightened his tie, and looked through the windscreen. 'A beautiful evening, I like the stars.'

He turned to Butter and raised an eyebrow. 'Can you move yet?'

The former Reach agent managed to curl the fingers of his right hand and the big toe on his left foot. He nodded.

'You may speak, but do so carefully. Some people have the ability to *hear* lies, but I can *smell* them. What did you do with the box Pip Duncan gave to you?'

'I kept it for him as a favour,' Butter admitted. 'But when he told me what it was, I wanted rid of it so I sold it as an ordinary role-playing game so it wouldn't be connected back to me.'

'You *sold* it?'

'Yes! To the first kid who came into my shop.'

'Who?'

'I don't know!'

'Then you will die.'

'P-please!'

'Talk, you parasite.'

'L-l-look, I know how to contact him!'

Heed looked from the syringe to Butter, and back again. Then he produced a mobile phone from his pocket. 'You can make one phone call. If I don't have a name and address at the end of it, then we're all going to find out how easy it is to make Butter melt.'

8

Danger

Christmas decorations were going up all over Mendlesham. It wouldn't be long before shops were empty, parents were broke and children were happy.

That was cool, though: Christmas was for little kids, after all.

Jake Cherish was drifting off to sleep when his mobile phone buzzed. He never rushed to check his messages because it was always Fatyak.

He yawned and turned over.

The phone buzzed again.

And again.

And again.

Jake reached across the bed and snatched it up. 'Fatyack,' he muttered. 'You better be dying ...'

The text was from 'Game Shop, JButt'. It said:

Jake. You have Pandora's Box. THE Pandora's Box. See Greek Myths if you don't know story.

Jake almost dropped the mobile. The air in the room felt a whole lot colder, and he found it quite hard to breathe. He swallowed twice, took a deep breath and checked the second text. It read:

The Reach are coming NOW. Bad people. Man they have hired will stop at nothing. He will kill you AND your friends.

Jake was holding the phone as if it might explode. He balled his other hand into a tight fist and began to thump himself on the top of the knee. The gesture usually helped him to think, but this time it couldn't stem the fear that overwhelmed him. If only Kellogg or Lemon were here, they'd know exactly what to do. He switched to the third text:

EVERYTHING that comes from box is evil: the magic within corrupts all who make use of the power!

Destroy the thing before it's too late!

Before his trembling fingers could completely succumb to the fear that gripped him, Jake clicked the fourth and final message. It just said:

RUN.

As the phone's battery alert started to beep, Jake looked down at his watch: in less than ten hours, it would be Christmas Eve. He plugged in his mobile to charge, then called the others and told them everything.

'We can't just give it back,' Kellogg said, his voice slightly distorted in the phone's mangled speaker. 'Besides, if this group will stop at nothing to get the box then the chances are they'll kill us for knowing about it anyway.'

'I agree with Kellogg!' Lemon didn't even wait for Jake to put his own opinion across. 'They'll kill us if we give it back, we know too much.'

Fatyak really didn't have a lot to add on the matter. 'They want the box?' he said. 'Let them come and get it.'

⚡

On the way up to her room, Lemon checked the hall telephone for messages and made a sickly face when there was one from her parents, assuring Melissa that they had landed safely. She took the sandwich plate to her room and switched on her laptop.

Jake's call about Stew Butter was on everyone's mind. She kept picturing the Outcasts in all sorts of terrible scenes, at the mercy of some unknown enemy.

After a few seconds spent cursing the slowness of her laptop's processor, she went on the internet and tried to find out about Pandora's Box.

The doorbell rang.

Lemon looked up from the laptop, and frowned. She checked the screen-clock, which read 10.08.

10.08 p.m. was a bit too late for visitors.

Melissa had taken her keys: she'd seen her pick them up from the stand.

Lemon lifted the laptop off her stomach and climbed out of bed. Hurrying across the landing outside her room, she tiptoed through her parents' bedroom and peeked around the edge of one of the plush curtains that covered the window.

She couldn't see who was standing at the door because the porch overhang always hid any visitors from view, but there was a car parked directly opposite her snowy drive. Two men were leaning against it, deep in conversation. From what little she could see, Lemon didn't like the look of them, and noted that the one on the left wouldn't have been out of place in a horror movie. She then saw a shadowy figure emerging from the front porch and sneaking off around the side of the house.

The doorbell rang a second time, and Lemon dashed back to her room. Changing from her pyjamas into a pair of jeans and a t-shirt, she quickly snatched up the laptop and spun it around.

Fatyak had left a message for her. It said, simply: HEY LEM.

She quickly tapped out a reply:

HELP ME – I THINK THEY'RE HERE.
GET Kellogg AND DEALMO. NOW.

Then she shut the laptop, pulled on a pair of trainers and dashed downstairs.

The ground floor of the house was silent, except for the occasional unnerving creak. Lemon saw that there was still a shadow at the front door and, dropping onto her hands and knees, she crawled towards the kitchen. When she arrived, snake-like, at the small step that separated the hall from the kitchen's lower level, she quickly slid into the room on her belly, causing Horace to look up from his basket in surprise.

'Shhh, Horace!' she whispered, suddenly afraid that the dog might break with tradition and bark at her. Fortunately, he went straight back to sleep.

From her position on the kitchen floor, Lemon could see that someone was peering through the conservatory window. The man was balding and his face was either lined or scarred: he certainly looked dangerous. Lemon observed that he was carrying a pack of some kind, and she gave a little gasp of horror when he started fiddling with the lock on the conservatory door.

Fortunately, he soon gave up and his shadow receded from the window.

Lemon took the opportunity to swivel herself around, and she crawled back into the hall corridor.

⚡

Kellogg climbed out onto his kitchen roof wearing a pair of camouflaged slacks and a baggy Hawaiian shirt. Fatyak thought he looked utterly ridiculous, but considering that *he* hadn't even managed to change out of his pyjamas, he supposed he was in no position to criticise.

The two friends hared off down

the street and dashed into the shadows of Preston Park.

'Did you call Dealmo?' Kellogg asked, setting the pace. He was running so fast that his voice came out in frantic fits and bursts.

'Couldn't get him,' Fatyak admitted, accelerating past his exhausted friend. 'His mobile just went to voicemail.'

⚡

Lemon stood at the window of Melissa's old room, which was positioned in the attic of the house and commanded the best view of the winter street outside.

A million different voices echoed in Lemon's head, but she remained at the window – transfixed – watching for movement. She wanted to run, she wanted to fight. She wanted to do a million things, yet her body simply wouldn't obey her.

The sound of breaking glass downstairs finally shook Lemon from her reverie. She tried to think clearly for a moment, and immediately realised she needed to go back to the lounge. There was a sturdy poker in a stand beside the fireplace. It wasn't exactly the most powerful weapon in the universe, but it was the closest thing she had to a sword. Jake's suggestion that she would be skilled with a sword seemed highly probable to her.

It was time to take a stand.

⚡

When Sluddy arrived at the conservatory door, Claxon had already busted the glass with a heavy crowbar and snaked his hand inside to spring the door lock.

'I got the boss's stuff from the car,' the giant thug boomed. 'Fell over a fair bit, though. I hate snow, that side path's a death trap.' He looked around. 'Where's the boss?'

'Here,' said Heed, moving past

Claxon and stepping into the house. 'You two search the house ... I'm going around the back.'

⚡

'Dealmo!'

Jake peered up from the tree hollow he'd been crouching in to see Kellogg and Fatyak standing over him. They were both out of breath.

'What's going on?' Kellogg managed.

'There are three of them,' said Jake, trying to sound more relaxed than he felt. 'I haven't been here long, but I saw them moving around the front garden.' He pointed at the side of the house. 'Fatyak, can you get to the box, like, *fast*?'

'Sure, I'll try.'

'Good. Kellogg; you need to stay with me – Lemon will probably need *major* help.'

The three friends split up: Jake and Kellogg heading one way and Fatyak dashing off in the opposite direction.

9

Confrontation

'Get out of my house.'

Heed's thug Sluddy looked up in surprise, just as Claxon staggered into the room behind him.

Lemon had appeared at the doorway that led from the kitchen into the conservatory. She was carrying an iron poker.

'Get *out* of my house,' she repeated, tightening her grip on the instrument with one hand while using the other to switch on the conservatory lights.

'You want to put that down, little girl,' Claxon warned, drawing a silver sword from a camouflaged sheath of his back. 'That's not a toy you've got there, and if you try anything with it, one of us is gonna get hurt. I'll cut a long story short for you – it's not gonna be me.'

Lemon didn't take her eyes off the man, which was difficult as she could also see his scarred companion creeping around the walls toward her.

Rather than stepping back from the advancing agents, Lemon decided that aggression would serve her better and took a step forward.

'Tell your friend to stay still, or I'll do it for both of you,' she snapped.

'Kids these days,' Claxon muttered, as Sluddy continued to advance on the girl. 'All mouth and no respect.'

'Oh dear,' said Lemon, fully aware that the scarred intruder was buying time for his trained ogre. 'And I tend not to have any respect for people who break into my house in the middle of the night. *If he moves one more inch I will throw this.*'

'Go ahead.' Claxon grinned, a smile that spread over his face like warm treacle. 'But I warn you, goldilocks, it will only make him mad.'

'Yeah,' echoed Sluddy, now directly

opposite. 'An' you won't like me when I'm ma-aaargh!'

Lemon had thrown the poker with such force that it sent the big man crashing into a glass cabinet on the far wall. She felt a fleeting pang of delight as the cabinet exploded: her parents would be furious. However, the feeling was short-lived.

Momentarily caught off-guard, Claxon quickly came to his senses and lunged for the girl, who caught hold of him mid-way through the dive and sent him careering over the tabletop. As he spilled over the edge of the table, Claxon snatched out a hand to aid his fall, and grabbed the big bag by mistake. Amid a clatter of swords, chains and breaking glass, he remembered the contents of Heed's arsenal and leapt off the floor, just as a pair of identical green snakes slithered from the depths of the bag. They were followed by a blue scorpion, and a miniature war erupted on the conservatory floor. Claxon looked as though he had turned to Irish dance in an effort to avoid the spitting snakes. He jigged and skipped his way around them, miraculously avoiding the pair just seconds before the scorpion engaged them.

Lemon was quick to spot the danger.

She retreated to the safety of the kitchen, ushering Horace inside and slamming the kitchen door just as Sluddy yanked the poker from his shoulder and, growling like an angry bear, stormed after her.

She ran through the corridor towards the hall, driving Horace before her as if she were herding a flock of wayward sheep. Fortunately, Horace was more co-operative than usual, which might have been down to the snake. Lemon took the stairs two at a time, suddenly realising that she had no plan of action other than to get away from the pair of thugs now pursuing her.

As she reached the first landing,

Sluddy charged along the corridor, swung round on the grand banister and launched himself up the stairs behind her. He looked absolutely incensed.

Lemon grabbed Horace's collar, dragged him into her parents' bedroom and slammed the door. Then she turned and made a run for the next floor, but Sluddy grabbed hold of her arm, slamming her into the wall with such force that she felt the mounted lamps crack and the picture frames fly off their nails.

'Look what you done,' Sluddy growled, slapping his injured shoulder and snatching a handful of Lemon's hair. 'You're gonna pay for that.'

He reeled back and slammed a fist towards the girl's jaw, but she was no longer there and his knuckles met the panelling with a loud crack. Surprised at the strength she had mustered to wrench herself away from the brute, Lemon quickly followed her evasive dodge with a swift knee, driving it straight into Sluddy's stomach. As the giant doubled up, she grabbed hold of his cannonball head and drove it in the direction of the storage heater with all her might. Getting a feel for her increased strength, she quickly lifted the stunned brute and threw him down onto the landing, where he moaned loudly before trying and failing to get to his feet.

Lemon looked down at him, and grinned. 'By the way, you punch like a little girl.'

ϟ

Fatyak moved silently through the trees, keeping to the perimeter of the high brick wall as he circled the house. He could see some sort of activity going on in the conservatory, but the garden itself was silent and wreathed in shadows. Dashing across the snow-covered grass, Fatyak threw himself into a variety of somersaults in order to stay low to the ground. It was only when he'd reached the rose bush where the box was buried that he realised someone was walking up and down inside the tree-house.

I'm a thief, he thought. *Not a fighter. They have their job and I have mine.*

Fatyak didn't waste another second. Instead, he dropped to his knees and began to scramble in the snow-covered dirt beside the rose bush, his hands working so frantically that he looked like a dog digging a hole for a bone. He had to stop every few seconds in order to rub his hands together for warmth.

Faster, Fatyak told himself.

Need to find it.

Eventually, his fingers scraped the edge of the box, and he heaved a huge sigh of relief, dragging it out of the dirt and rolling over onto his knees in an attempt to leap away.

Nathan Heed landed on his back like a giant spider.

10

A Bad Wish

Claxon stumbled out of the house, one hand probing the collar of his shirt while the other felt around his lower back. Despite the fact that he could still make out the snakes and the scorpion circling each other on the conservatory floor, he was convinced that something with more legs than eyes was crawling up his back.

As he staggered over the lawn, Jake and Kellogg exploded from the edge of the trees and smashed into him.

Claxon fell back under the combined weight of the boys, but recovered enough to deliver a punch that split Jake's lip and sent him flying sideways. Kellogg used the opportunity to slam his own elbow into Claxon's jaw, which turned out to be a mistake causing an incredible amount of pain.

'Had a fair few knocks on my jawbone,' the thug spat, snatching hold of Kellogg's head and driving his face into the dirt. 'That's why they took it out a few years ago and replaced it with a steel mesh.' He leaned heavily on Kellogg's neck, but released his grip when Jake staggered back into the fray, delivering a well-aimed kick to the small of his back. Claxon cried out in fury, then leapt to his feet, spun around and punched Jake square in the face.

Kellogg scrambled to his feet and started to run, but Claxon was surprisingly quick. He swept the lanky youth's feet out from under him and brought the boy crashing back to the ground. Then he put two hands around Kellogg's neck ...

Sluddy crashed down another flight of stairs and crumpled to a heap on the hall floor. Lemon stepped down after him, heaving the big man onto his back and dragging him around the hat-stand.

'Thanks for visiting,' she said, unlocking the front door before reaching down and wrenching the giant back onto his feet. 'Do come again.' Sluddy landed on the front drive, his face covered in blood and his eyes staring up at the stars in a dream-like daze.

Lemon slammed the door after him, and turned her attention to the back of the house.

⚡

Pandora's Box soared over the snow, spinning in the air several times before it landed with a thud in a thick mound of icy dirt.

Nathan Heed slammed an open palm towards Fatyak's exposed neck, gasping with astonishment when the chubby kid shirked the blow and slipped between his legs as deftly as a boy half his size. No stranger to stealth, Heed used the tree trunk to kick himself into the air, performed a perfect black flip and landed on Fatyak's back. At least, that was the plan. When he actually landed, his arms and legs braced for the greatest possible impact, Fatyak was already several feet away, snatching the box from the dirt mound as he dashed back toward the house.

Heed leapt to his feet and hurtled after him.

⚡

Claxon tightened his grip around Kellogg's throat, grinning spitefully as the skinny youth began to lose consciousness.

'Don't like *that*, do you?' he snarled, glancing back briefly to check that the second kid was still out for the count. On the other side of the garden, he saw Nathan Heed pursuing an overweight teenager who was moving at a surprising speed and carrying – *the box!*

Claxon released his grip on

Kellogg's neck and jumped to his feet, just as Lemon cannoned into him.

A few yards away, Nathan Heed had put on an incredible burst of speed and had managed to catch Fatyak before he entered the house. He was not the Reach's best agent for nothing. The two of them were now struggling madly over the box, Heed regularly overpowering Fatyak only to find that his most devastating blows were missing their mark. For his part, Fatyak dodged and weaved with all his borrowed skill, leaping every leg-sweep and weaving his head around the agent's calculated strikes as though he were trained in every martial art known to man.

On the grass, Claxon was having considerable trouble with Lemon. None of his previous encounters quite prepared him for trading punches with a ridiculously strong, possibly insane teenage girl. Whatever *was* wrong with the girl, she was taking every strike he mustered and returning each shot with twice the energy. Claxon staggered as yet another iron fist slammed into the side of his steel jaw.

He spat on the ground and made one last, desperate lunge, but once again Lemon was ready for him. She side-stepped the thug's attack, planting a fist in his stomach as he careered past. Then she took a run up, leapt into the air and drop-kicked him between the shoulder blades. Claxon screamed out as he flew head-first through the kitchen window and landed in a shower of glass on the lino flooring.

⚡

Heed circled Fatyak warily, looking for an opening. One *opportunity* was all he needed to put the boy down, one momentary lapse of concentration and the box would be in his grasp.

The icy snow crunched beneath their feet.

'You've used it,' Heed muttered,

his gaze flicking to the box and back to Fatyak. 'You're far too big to move the way you do ... that box has given you an advantage of some kind. Do you know what it is, my *fat* little friend? Do you know what that box can *gift* you? All the world to choose from and *you* ask for quick reactions!'

'Who *are* you?'

'My name is Nathan Heed, and mine is the last face you will ever see. Does that scare you?'

Fatyak held onto the box as though he'd given birth to it, his chubby fingers closed around the edges so tightly that the ends were turning white.

'At the very least you could have asked to drop a stone or two,' Heed persisted, his eyes still searching Fatyak's for weakness. 'Or are you holding out the hope that all this magical ducking and diving will shed the three tyres you have strapped to your gut?'

Fatyak launched himself at the agent, making his first and last mistake. Heed didn't even attempt to dodge out of the way; he simply targeted a chop at Fatyak's throat and caught the box before the kid hit the ground.

'I'll take that,' he muttered, leaping over Fatyak's prone body and springing the catch on the front of the box.

He threw back the lid, revealing the box's hand-shaped interior.

Hmm ... how interesting.

Heed drove his hand into the box, closed his eyes and said in a loud voice.

'Immortality.'

After all, he thought. *Who could wish for anything more?*

11

Endgame

The snow-covered house and its frosty garden had become a place of utter chaos. While Sluddy lay dreaming on the front drive, Claxon slept off the beating of his life on the cold lino of the kitchen floor. In the rear garden, Jake and Kellogg were lost in a world of their own dark dreams, while Lemon marched determinedly across the lawn, her cool blue eyes locked on Nathan Heed.

'You,' she said, raising an

accusatory finger at the agent. 'Drop that box, right now – you're not leaving with it. I'm serious, don't make the same mistake your friends did.'

'Mistake?' said Heed, looking down at the box as he snapped it shut. 'I don't think I've made any particular mistakes *here*. Hmm ...' He gestured towards Fatyak. 'Are you as fast as your lardy friend?'

Lemon shook her head. 'No, but I'm twice as strong. Do as you're told – put the box *down*.'

'I think not.' Heed flashed a smile that actually made Lemon feel sick. 'If you are so strong, little girl, why don't you come over here and *prove it*.'

Lemon gritted her teeth, and charged. However, she had only reached the halfway mark between herself and the agent when he did something that she really hadn't been expecting.

He hurled the box at her.

Caught off-guard, Lemon quickly changed direction and threw up her arms to catch it, leaping back like a professional rugby player intercepting the pass of the century.

Nathan Heed immediately seized the opportunity and sprang forward. Snatching hold of the back of Lemon's t-shirt, he produced a syringe from the depths of his coat and plunged it straight into her exposed neck.

She let out a cry of pain, dropped the box she'd managed to snatch from the air and turned on Heed like an angry lion. Her fury at the attack was so great that she'd picked up the agent and pitched him across the garden before she even thought to pull the needle from her throat.

Heed flew through the air as if he'd been launched from a cannon, crashing into the side of the tree-house and plummeting to the ground with a series of disgusting cracks. To Lemon's astonishment, the man promptly got straight back to his feet, laughing hysterically.

She shook her head and looked down at the syringe in her hands. It looked old-fashioned, almost an antique, in fact. The central tube contained a measure of green liquid. Looking at it, Lemon estimated that approximately half of the dose had been administered. She looked up again, but the entire garden had become an indistinct blur.

Pain was rising inside her, coursing through her veins with remarkable speed. Every nerve in her body exploded with agony.

She tried to scream, but no sound

left her lips. Lemon staggered slightly and, as her arms and legs began to shake with a violent, uncontrollable energy, she collapsed on the icy lawn and began to fit.

'It's an interesting sensation, I imagine?' said Heed, as he made his way towards the fallen girl, moving his head from side to side as the various bones in his neck reset themselves. 'I believe the Fishaun Indians called it Mahiouki and used it to kill their most despised enemies.' He crouched down beside Lemon and picked up the box. 'Oh dear, your incredible *strength* will delay the full effects of the poison. It could take *hours* to finish you off.'

Heed checked the box for any damage that went beyond the superficial, and found none. Glancing around the garden one last time, he gave a contented nod and headed for the snow-covered gravel path that led around the side of the house.

Unfortunately, the path was blocked. Heed looked up at a sight that actually forced him to hesitate.

'If she dies, *you* die.'

Jake was standing in the middle of the path, his eyes blazing red and his lips curled in a bitter snarl. He was encased in a ball of pure blue energy.

'You can't kill me,' Heed said, taking an uneasy step back. 'I've used the box, just like you. I'm immortal.'

Lightening swirled around Jake's body, causing Heed to stand and stare in fascinated horror as the electricity began to draw into sharp focus. When Jake raised his hand and pointed directly at Heed, the lightning poured through him like water being directed through a funnel. It flashed across the garden, hitting the Reach agent with such force that it lifted him clean off his feet. The box flew out of Heed's hands and tumbled over the snow.

Jake stepped forward with

increased confidence, guiding the lightning as it continued to course through and around Nathan Heed. Screaming with rage, he stretched his fingers until they ached with the electric power that was spilling from them. When he could bear the strain no more, he let his hands drop to his sides and allowed his mind to relax.

Nathan Heed plummeted from the sky and landed with a loud thud in a mud patch on the edge of the garden. His face and hands were charred, and his clothes were smoking.

Jake muttered something under his

breath, and crunched through the snow towards the agent.

⚡

Still holding a hand to his aching temple, Kellogg staggered across the icy lawn and dropped onto his knees beside Lemon's twitching body. The girl's eyes had filled with tears and her mouth was moving in a silent cry for help.

Kellogg reached down and took Lemon into his arms, supporting her head with one hand and gently lifting her shoulders with the other. As he tried to focus all his energy on healing his friend, he found – to his surprise – that he was crying himself. Kellogg had cried many times since his father died, but these tears felt different. They literally flowed down his cheeks.

'D-don't die, Lem,' he said, cursing himself for his failure to defeat the thug who'd choked him unconscious. Through a haze of tears, Kellogg's eyes found the syringe. Still gripping Lemon's trembling shoulders in one hand, he quickly scanned her arms and neck for any signs of the needle's entry. The wound was immediately obvious, a tiny crater of puffed skin circled a pinprick on the left side of her neck.

Kellogg closed his fingers around the injury, and focussed his attention on drawing out the poison. As he tightened his grip on Lemon's neck, he felt the warm energy flowing through him.

'I couldn't save my dad!' he said, trying to hold his nerve as the tears swam down his cheeks. 'But I can save you, Lem. I can and I *will*. Out! Out! Ouuuuut!'

Kellogg closed his eyes and raised his head to the heavens as the power built inside him. He was so consumed with determination to heal Lemon that he didn't even feel the green liquid pouring over his fingers.

'K-k-Kellogg?'

Lemon's eyes flickered open, and she tried to raise herself up off the ground. Kellogg released his hold on her – the flesh on her neck melted together and the needle wound faded away – he hugged his friend with every ounce of the strength he had left.

ϟ

Jake thundered towards Nathan Heed, his eyes fixed on the fallen agent as he muttered an incantation and conjured a spinning fireball in his hand.

You're not dead, Jake thought, bitterly. *I just know it.*

Sure enough, Heed was soon back on his feet, patting his clothes in several places and laughing.

'That really hurt,' he said, stumbling a little as the boy advanced on him. 'Congratulations. I think that may be the first time anyone has ever caused me pain.'

Jake shrugged. 'I haven't started yet,' he said, raising his hand.

Heed dropped his gaze to the ball of red flame in the boy's palm.

'I told you – I'm immortal. Do you understand what that means? You can't kill me. But I can kill you. It doesn't matter how much of that cartoon magic you use, or how much pain you inflict ... sooner or later, you'll get tired, and when you do I'll strike you down without a *hint* of mercy.'

Jake nodded. 'Good job I'm not tired yet.' He threw out his hand and sent a ball of fire slamming into Nathan Heed, who screamed and staggered backwards, wreathed in flame.

'Arghghghgh!'

Jake watched the agent dive onto the ground and roll back and forth in a frantic attempt to put himself out. Then Jake muttered under his breath, and called forth a swarm of killer bees. He sent the swarm of insects hurtling towards Heed, who was quickly surrounded by a raging cloud of buzzing, stinging pain.

Amid the agent's cries of distress, Jake advanced. But he was moving a good deal slower now, and his hand held nothing more than air.

Ideas, he thought. *I'm running out of ideas.*

Jake took a deep breath, and tried to concentrate. He was also running out of energy: he could feel the fatigue mounting inside him. A small part of his mind yearned to create more punishment for the immortal agent, but his body just wanted to lie down and sleep for a fortnight.

Nathan Heed emerged from the swarm cloud covered in sickening welts. He staggered towards Jake, his skin beginning to heal even as he spat a plethora of curses at the boy.

'Is that all you've got?' the agent demanded. 'The lightning hurt, I'll grant you. Even the fire had a certain kick to it! But bees? Has your mind run *dry*, you little punk?'

Heed picked up his pace and charged at Jake, drawing a needle thin dagger as the boy shrank before him.

Jake threw out his hand, but no energy was released from it. Heed smashed into him and the pair crashed into the snow.

'Taste death, kid,' screamed the agent, forcing his hand toward Jake's throat as the boy grabbed Heed's wrist and fought with all his might.

'Heed.'

The dagger a quarter of an inch from his throat, Jake's resistance was waning.

'Heed!'

The knife edge kissed the flesh of Jake's exposed neck.

'HEEEEEEEEEEEEEEEEEEEEEEEEED!'

Nathan Heed glanced up to find the source of the scream, and saw the chubby boy walking across the roof of the house. He was carrying the box.

Fatyak paused on the crest of the roof, and began to slip and slide his way down the frosted tiles, faltering several times until his feet found the firmer ground of the bathroom roof.

'You know what?' he yelled, 'People like you have always called me names.'

He walked to the very edge of the roof, and stuck his hand inside the box. 'I used to pretend it didn't hurt, but it does and I wish it would stop.' Fatyak let out a heavy sigh, and teetered on the edge of the bathroom roof. 'You know what else I wish, Mr Heed? I wish this box of yours was *really* fragile.'

As Heed looked on with mounting

horror, Fatyak raised both hands above his head.

'I'm not fat,' he shouted. 'I'm BIG-BONED!'

He hurled the box at the ice-covered patio, where it shattered into a thousand pieces, sending out a bolt of pure blue energy that coursed through all five of the garden's stunned inhabitants. Fatyak slipped and stumbled across the roof, Lemon leaned on Kellogg for strength and the healer felt relieved that he'd helped his friend before the box had been broken.

The power seeped out of them so abruptly that they experienced a moment of terrible weakness.

Fatyak felt as if every muscle and sinew in his body was paying the price for the incredible feats the box had enabled him to perform. Lemon felt like she was wading through glue: each movement she made was more difficult than the last. Kellogg had a sudden, terrifying pang of pain, as if a thousand wounds were opening in his body for every healing touch he had applied.

Dealmo, however, was focused on Heed.

As his last conjured fireball died in his hands, he saw his opportunity and charged, slamming into the agent like a rogue missile. When Heed went down, Jake followed him to the ground and, glancing a single, solitary punch off the man's pointed chin, knocked Nathan Heed out cold.

Only then did he succumb to the horrible, sinking sensation of being ... *ordinary*, and collapsed onto the grass.

Kellogg and Lemon staggered to his side, supporting each other in a sort of three-legged race.

Jake looked up at them. 'Call the police,' he said 'Tell them we had a break-in. If those idiots want to start talking about the box, let them: nobody will believe them anyway.'

Lemon made the call.

'What about the box?' Kellogg asked.

Jake raised himself onto his elbows, and reached across the grass for a lone splintered shard from the wooden wreckage. The piece had flown further than the rest of the shattered relic, and was wedged into a ground like a fractured dart.

'A keepsake,' he said, closing his fist around it. 'We should all keep a piece: something to tell our kids about … if we ever have any—'

'or if they'd believe us,' Lemon laughed, putting her phone away.

The group shared a glance, relief flooding over them all as their energy began to return.

'Now we've lost our powers,' said Fatyak, waddling across the snowy garden towards his friends. 'Do you think life will seem, you know, really boring?'

'Nah,' said Dealmo, smiling at Lemon. 'I reckon us Outcasts have earned a new reputation.'

'I can't believe you threw the box off the roof …' Kellogg smirked, glancing at Fatyak with a new respect. 'That was really, really brave, dude.'

Fatyak shrugged. 'I'm not sure what was going through my head, but somehow I just knew that the powers didn't make us, you know, *us*. It was like our friendship was stronger.'

'You got that right,' Lemon grinned. 'We've always been an awesome team, even when we were just a bunch of ... outcasts. The question is, what do we do for fun now that I can't throw cars around, Jake can't conjure massive frogs, Fatyak can't climb buildings and Kellogg can't make us all better when we get hurt?'

Jake stopped dead, and a slow smile spread across his face. 'I've got an idea,' he said. 'We can go back to doing what we *always* did for fun ...'

DAVID GRIMSTONE

Epilogue

Butter's Game shop on a Saturday morning might fail to put you in mind of a hive of hungry gamers, but every kid who found themselves picked last for football or walked most of Cross Country was there.

In one corner, Chang ran his magic tournament for a bunch of new kids, while beefy Hannah Jenkins challenged everyone who couldn't beat her at Uno to an impromptu arm wrestling tournament.

Jake, Lemon, Kellogg and Fatyak occupied their favourite table beside the window.

They were playing Zombie Horde, one they usually loved but none of them could concentrate on the game.

'I can't run ... *again*,' Fatyack moped. 'Being ordinary sucks.'

Lemon shrugged. 'Only when you've had a taste of something different, I guess. Besides, you did what none of us could do; you actually destroyed the box. Somehow, I can't see you as ordinary ... and I doubt the likes of Todd Miller will ever give us another problem.'

'Yeah,' Fatyack agreed. 'Crazy year, eh?'

'It all seems so unreal, now ... but I can still feel what it was like to *be* that strong.'

'The thing that worries me most,' Kellogg muttered, 'is that we only just beat the Reach and we were all practically indestructible. What happens if they decide we need to pay for destroying their box?'

'It's been two weeks,' Jake reminded them, only a trace of doubt in his voice. 'If they were going to come after us, they'd have done it by now, right?'

Lemon leaned back in her chair. 'What if Nathan Heed was just the tip of the iceberg?' she said. 'What if—'

'Sorry to interrupt.' The new Saturday boy at Butter's had sidled up to the table with a heavy box in his hand. 'A new game just came in. The boss said it's like Dungeon Chaos, but you get to play heroes and there's this—'

'Thanks,' Jake held up his hand and laughed. 'But go give it to Chang, we don't play those sorts of games anymore.'

As the boy with the box wandered off, Jake shared a nervous glance with his friends. 'At least,' he said. 'I hope we don't.'

ACKNOWLEDGMENTS

Thanks to Chiara Stone and Barbara Ann Stone
for reading and commenting on the manuscript,
Sophie Hicks for selling the book and Lauren Davis
for editing it. Special thanks to Anne McNeil for
her notes, her loyalty and her continued efforts
to fight my corner.